D1550747

LIBBY'S NEW GLASSES

WRITTEN AND ILLUSTRATED BY

Tricia Tusa

HOLIDAY HOUSE / NEW YORK

Library of Congress Cataloging in Publication Data

Tusa, Tricia.
Libby's new glasses.

SUMMARY: Libby can't accept the idea of wearing
glasses until she meets a lovely bird with the same
problem.
[1. Eyeglasses—Fiction]   I. Title.
PZ7.T8825Li   1984   [E]   83-26688
ISBN 0-8234-0523-0

This is for MARGERY and DAVID and
JOHN and KATE and BARBARA and CATHY,
with thanks

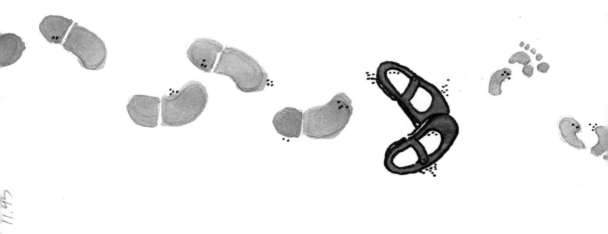

"Why me?" moaned Libby as she sat in the eye doctor's office after getting new glasses.

The eye doctor smiled a big smile and patted her head. "Wearing eyeglasses is not so bad. Cheer up," he said.

"What does he know?" thought Libby. "He just gives them out. He doesn't wear them."

When Libby arrived home, she ran to her room, locked her door, and stared at her new face in the mirror. "All the kids at school will tease me!" she cried. Right then she decided to run away from home and hide forever.

She secretly packed her things and snuck out the backdoor.

She walked through fields . . .

down roads . . .

through woods . . .

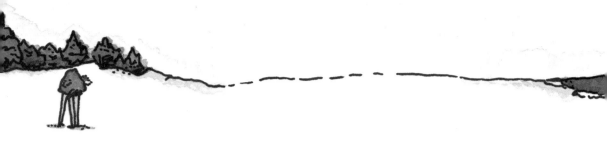

. . . and finally arrived on a beach, hot and tired.
She spotted something in the distance and squinted.
She couldn't recognize what it was.

"What's that?" she wondered. "Maybe it's a tree or an umbrella. Maybe I could sit under it and rest. It looks nice and shady."

Libby took out her glasses and put them on. She recognized legs and feathers.

"Why, it's a bird, and its head is in the sand!" she gasped.

She went over to it. "Do you need help?" she asked.
"Rmpff," said the bird.

Libby began pulling on its neck. A garbled voice full of sand squawked, "What do you think you're doing? Let go of me!"

"A head must be attached to that long neck of yours," said Libby. "So why have you buried it in the sand?"
"I'm hiding," said the bird.

"Why?" asked Libby.
"If you must know," said the bird,
"because I'm embarrassed."

"Embarrassed!" exclaimed Libby. "Why should you be embarrassed?"

"None of your business," said the bird.

"You don't have any reason to be embarrassed," said Libby. "You have beautiful feathers and a soft, fuzzy tail!"

"Thank you," mumbled the bird.

"And your legs are so long, I bet you could
run faster than the fastest runner in my class!"
exclaimed Libby.

"My, my," said the bird.

"And, oh boy! You must be really tall when you hold your head up!" cried Libby.

For a moment, the bird forgot it was embarrassed.
It lifted its head
out of the sand.

What a surprise! On its beak was
a shiny new pair of eyeglasses.
"Wow!" said Libby. "You have new
eyeglasses, too!"

Quickly, the bird stuffed its head back in the sand.
"Now you know why I'm hiding," it mumbled.

"You're silly. Your eyeglasses look great. You have
no reason to hide," Libby said.

"Really?" asked the bird.

"Really," answered Libby.

The bird slowly pulled its head out from the sand.
It ruffled its feathers and
began to strut around.

"Thank you," it said. "You don't look so bad in
glasses yourself."

"I don't?" asked Libby.

"No," said the bird. "In fact, your eyeglasses are very becoming."

"They are?" asked Libby.

"Sure!" said the bird.

"Let's take a walk," said Libby. "Maybe things
will look different through our new glasses."

So Libby and the bird walked and walked.

They saw starfish. And seashells. And sailboats.
And fish jumping.

And a sunset.
Everything looked clearer through their new glasses.

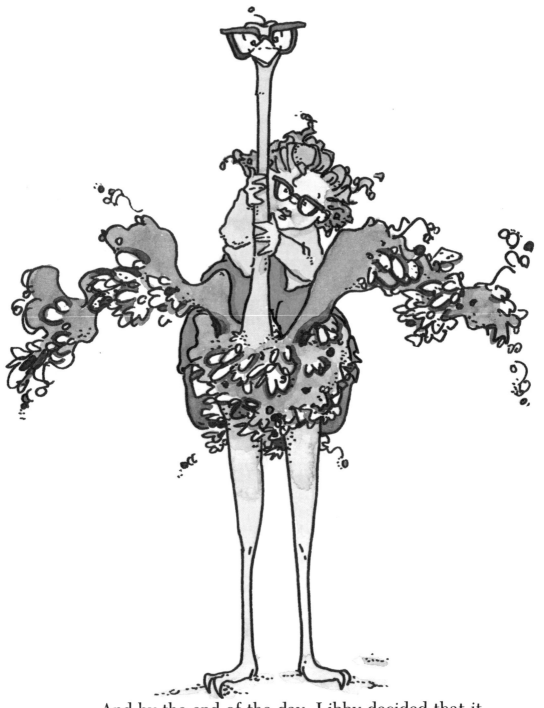

And by the end of the day, Libby decided that it wasn't so bad to have eyeglasses after all.

DUE

MA

AUG